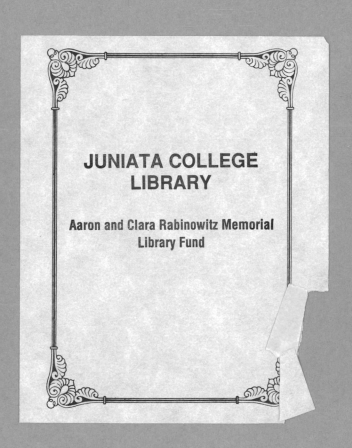

A WAGONLOAD OF FISH

TRANSLATED AND ADAPTED BY
JUDIT Z. BODNÁR

ILLUSTRATED BY
ALEXI NATCHEV

LOTHROP, LEE & SHEPARD BOOKS   NEW YORK

ONCE THERE WAS, OR ONCE THERE WASN'T, there was once an old peasant. He and his beetle-browed wife owned their own small cottage. Behind it lay a vegetable garden, and beyond that, decent pasture land. Their oxen were old, but still strong and willing. They had a generous milk cow, a sow that bore a litter every year, a hog, and three dozen pullets. So they had plenty of peas and tomatoes, carrots and potatoes, cheese and butter, bacon and hocks, eggs and broth, and now and again a crisp roast or chicken paprikás.

The peasant would have been a satisfied man had it not been for his wife. For years she had complained that the cottage was too small and shabby, that her clothing was drab and dowdy, that her husband was shiftless and lazy. For years the old man had merely nodded and gone about his business.

Then one December the wife decided that she could not bear to eat cheese or butter, bacon or hocks, eggs or broth or roasts anymore. The only thing that would please her delicate, refined palate, she declared, was fish.

"Fish!" cried the peasant. "It is the dead of winter. The fishing pond and all the streams are frozen solid. Even Lake Balaton is covered with ice four inches thick!"

"Well, I shouldn't have expected anything from *you* anyhow," said the wife.

From then on, the woman could think of nothing but fish. In January and February, she embroidered codfish on all the napkins and tablecloths. In March and April, she baked all the bread in the shape of mackerel. In May, she hummed *The Pearl Fisher* day and night—it was the only song she knew that had anything to do with fish.

The old man tried to ignore her. But no matter where he cast his eyes, all he saw was fish. The birds on the budding branches looked like flying fish. The snuffling piglets looked for all the world like fat brown carp. His wife's curls swam on her head like gray fingerlings and she smelled like cod liver oil. Every night the old man dreamed of trout and halibut and herring.

By mid-June he could bear it no longer. He gathered his poles and hooks and three seining nets and flung them into the wagon, then set off through the woods.

Now, at the far edge of that woods there lived a fox. Like every fox, he was sly and devious and loved to eat. On midsummer's night he was very hungry indeed. But though he searched from dusk to dawn, from here to there and everywhere, he could not find even a morsel to eat. By the time the sun began to yawn and open its eyes, the fox felt faint. His stomach rumbled and growled. His paws ached and his tail drooped. He dragged himself to the side of the road and collapsed beneath a prickly black raspberry bush.

Suddenly the smell of fish clapped him on the nose. He picked up his head, pricked up his ears, and squinted up and down the road. What should he see but the old peasant's two brown oxen pulling a cloth-draped wagon. The closer the wheels rolled, the stronger the fishy odor became and the farther the fox's long, red tongue hung down.

The fox slunk out from under the bush, sidled into the road, and stretched across the wagon ruts. He arranged his rust-red plume just so. Then he lay as still as a fallen sapling.

When the peasant saw the fox lying right in his path, he called out to his oxen—"Ho! Ho, now!"—and the beasts halted. The old man stepped down from his wagon, leaned over, and took a good close look and a good long sniff. The fox wasn't breathing.

"Hmmm. Pearly, look at this. How the devil could this fine-looking creature have come to his end right here in the middle of the road?" he muttered. "Bimbi, have you ever seen such a fine foxtail? *Tyu,* what a beautiful stole his hide will make for my wife! With a fox stole and a whole wagonload of fish, she'll never have reason to nag me again!"

Then, grasping the fox by the neck, he dragged him over to the wagon and tossed him in. "*Tchaa,* Pearly! *Tchaa,* Bimbiko! Be on your way," he shouted. And the oxen started slowly down the road through the woods with the peasant plodding beside them.

The moment the wheels began to turn, the fox took a long, deep breath. Then he began to shove the fish out of the wagon. While the man prodded his oxen and mumbled to them and the wagon creaked and groaned, the fish dropped from the wagon bed one after the other.

When the wagon reached the edge of the woods, the fox leaped
out and ran down the roadside, gobbling fish at every step.

The old man drove right up to the door. "Wife, come quickly! Look at what I brought you—a lovely fox and a *hundred pounds* of fish!"

But when his wife came out, she saw only a handful of fish and no fox at all. She scolded him soundly for being too lazy to fill the wagon.

The poor man saw that it was true. The fox and most of his catch were gone. *"Tyu!"* he whispered, gazing at his wife and shaking his head as he slowly unyoked the oxen.

"The pond was so peaceful and quiet....Pearly, Bimbiko, have you ever wondered what reindeer meat tastes like? With you two, a hunting trip to Lapland could take *months*!"

And the old man smiled as he fed the oxen and went about his business.

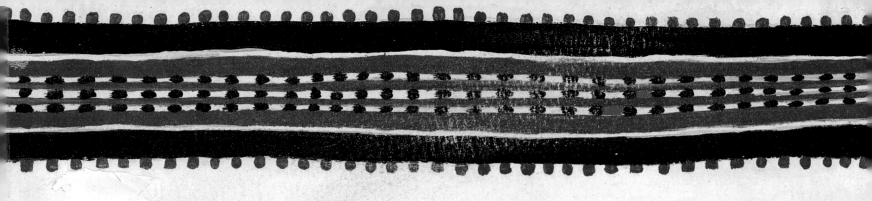

AUTHOR'S NOTE

THIS STORY stems from the first half of a Hungarian folktale about a very greedy and ingenious fish-loving fox. I loved hearing and reading it as a young child and, later, telling it to my two children. Among other sources, the original can be found in a book called *Creánga Mesék,* published in Budapest by Móra Kieado shortly before or after World War II.

Lake Balaton, 48 miles long, is the largest lake in Europe and lies in the western part of Hungary—about 2,200 miles from Lapland.

To Morgan,
who would have painted a wooden fish
and broken a lot of teeth
—JZB

For Marti, my nephew
—AN

Library of Congress Cataloging in Publication Data
Bodnár, Judit Z. A Wagonload of Fish / translated and adapted by
Judit Z. Bodnár; illustrated by Alexi Natchev.
p.   cm.   Summary: A peasant who tries to satisfy his wife by catching a
wagonload of fish is outsmarted by a fox.
ISBN 0-688-12172-1. — ISBN 0-688-12173-X (lib. bdg.)
[1. Folklore—Hungary.] I. Natchev, Alexi, ill. II. Title.
III. Title: Wagonload of Fish. PZ8.1.B5885Wag 1993
[398.21]—dc20   93-19047 CIP AC